More Than Spots & Stripes

BRAVE
BOOKS

DOM-A-TRON

THE OLD ISLANDS

Doomsdome

Burrycanter

UTOPIA

Freedom Island

WIGGAMORE WOO

SUMA SAVANNA

Rushington

Hive Hav

Furenzy Park

Toke-A-Toke

Wonder Well

Capitol

RAKA RAIN FOREST

Mushroom Village

Deserted Desert

Mt. Avalerif

Sky Tree

Snapfast Meadow

CAR-A-LAGO COAST

Starlotte City

Gray Landing

Home of the Brave

Welcome to Freedom Island, Home of the Brave, where good battles evil and truth prevails. It's up to you to defend our great nation. Save the animals of Furenzy Park by completing the BRAVE Challenge at the end of this book.

Watch this video for an introduction to the story and BRAVE universe!

Saga One: The Origins

Book 3

More than Spots & Stripes

Shivermore

Nogard Cavern

MONOCK MOUNTAINS

Meltonville

CABAL ISLAND

Temple of The Serpent

Saga One: The Origins—Book 3

More than Spots & Stripes

Copyright © 2021 by BRAVE BOOKS
All Rights Reserved

Book Illustrations © 2021 by Ali Elzeiny
Map Illustration © 2021 by Ali Elzeiny

Published by BRAVE BOOKS
www.BRAVEbooks.com

ISBN: 978-1-955550-61-1 (paperback)

First edition published in the USA in 2021 by BRAVE BOOKS

Printed in the USA

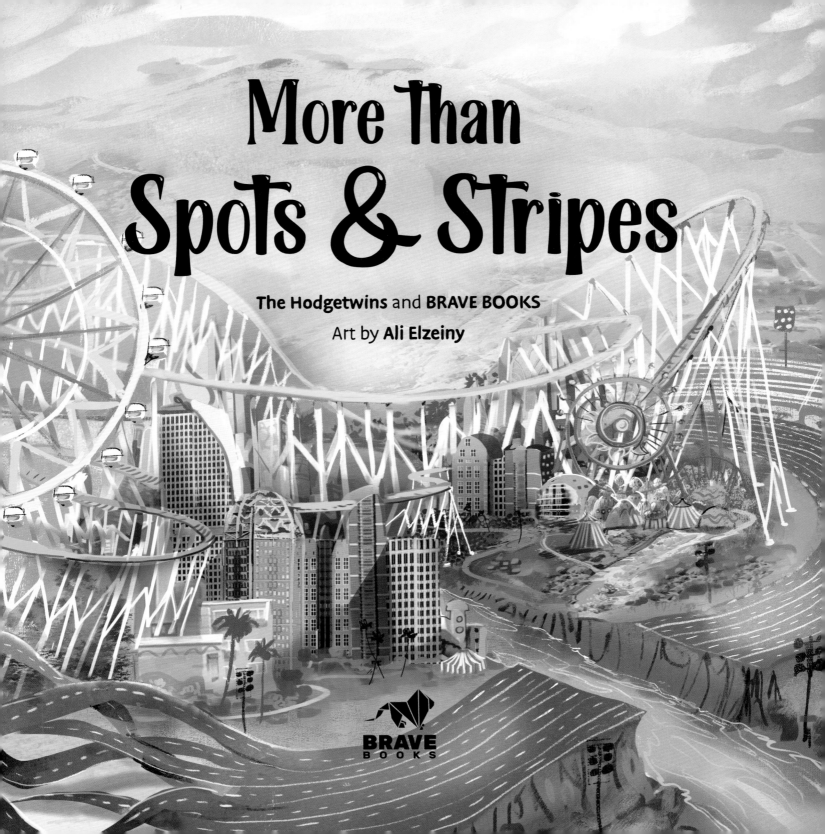

More than
Spots & Stripes

The Hodgetwins and **BRAVE BOOKS**

Art by **Ali Elzeiny**

BRAVE
BOOKS

When Rebel was an itty bitty cub, she used to go with her granny to watch the cheetahs run. As she watched, her heart beat eagerly, pitter-patter pitter-patter, against her spots. "One day," she would say to Granny, "I'm going to race on the big track."

Then Granny would give Rebel a kiss on the top of her head and say, "If you work very hard, my dear, one day you will."

When Rebel grew bigger, she joined Furenzy Racing School. There, she met Madi, her teammate, and they spent years practicing together.

They learned to run and leap and sprint as fast as they could. More
importantly, they learned that racing on the big track took very hard work.
Rebel didn't mind because she knew the hard work made her strong.

At the end of her last year at school, the best racers in all of
Freedom Island came to visit. They planned to race Rebel and her
classmates to show them what it was like on the big track. As
Rebel waited for the race at the end of the week, she felt her heart
beat nervously, ba-dum ba-dum, against her spots.

A striped cheetah named Bella, the most famous racer of all, gave a speech to help the students prepare. "When striped cheetahs built Furenzy Race Track many years ago, they hated spotted cheetahs. As they ran, the Stripes would throw banana peels to make the Spots trip on the track."

Rebel nodded, remembering Granny's stories of the cheating striped cheetahs.

"Even though Stripes don't throw banana peels anymore," said Bella, "every single striped cheetah still wants the Spots to lose. The Stripes are all still cheaters."

Rebel cocked her head. "If racers aren't breaking rules, how are they cheating?"

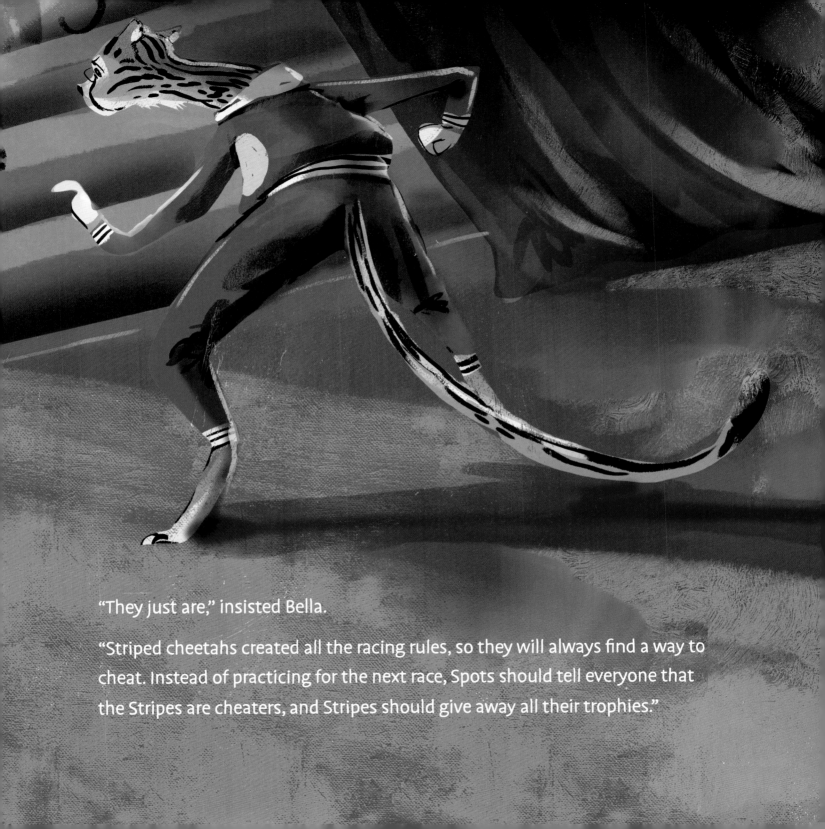

"They just are," insisted Bella.

"Striped cheetahs created all the racing rules, so they will always find a way to cheat. Instead of practicing for the next race, Spots should tell everyone that the Stripes are cheaters, and Stripes should give away all their trophies."

The next morning, when Madi strolled outside for breakfast, Rebel stopped her, holding back tears.

"Why are you cheating and trying to make spotted cheetahs like me lose? I thought we were friends, but Bella says you hate me!"

"Excuse me, I am not cheating," protested Madi.

"I'm your teammate and your friend! Bella is a liar, and if you believe her, you're as foolish as she is. If you don't trust me, you can find yourself another teammate."

For the rest of the week, the school was split. The spotted students stopped practicing to yell that the Stripes made racing unfair.

The striped cheetah students stopped practicing to yell that the Spots were crybabies. Only the older, famous cheetahs continued to prepare for the big race.

When the students finally ran against the famous racers, not a single one did well. After a week of not practicing, they huffed and puffed down the track. By the time they made it to the final lap, they were tired and slow. Rebel came in last, and she was sure it was all Madi's fault.

Rebel pouted on the way back to the locker, until she heard a familiar voice.

"My plan has worked! Even though I am old and slower than these young cheetahs, my words distracted them from training. Because they're no longer working hard, we won today, and we will win the Furenzy Fifty-Three."

The Furenzy Fifty-Three was the biggest race of the year, and Rebel had dreamed her whole life of winning it. But Bella was right. If Rebel didn't keep working hard, she would never win the Furenzy Fifty-Three.

Sprinting back to the track, Rebel found her friend.
"Madi, I'm sorry I blamed you for cheating when
you hadn't done anything wrong."

"I forgive you," said Madi, giving Rebel a hug, "and I'm sorry too. I should have listened to you and realized you were hurt."

From then on, Rebel and Madi didn't join their classmates in the yelling but practiced every day.

Rebel realized that she would win or lose by the choices she made, not whether she had spots or stripes. And from now on, she would choose her friends based on how they treated her.

She and Madi ran and leapt and sprinted together, and most importantly, they learned to love and help each other again.

Now that Rebel and Madi finished racing school, it was time for the Furenzy Fifty-Three ....

Rebel recovered from the banana peel nimbly,
strong from weeks of practice with Madi.

Racing around the last turn, she and Bella strained, neck-and-neck, towards the finish line. Stretching and reaching, Rebel jumped!

"Friends," Rebel announced, "we can never win by hating and blaming each other. Even though Stripes have hurt me and other Spots, we can't fix anything by hurting them back and calling them names."

"We are more than our spots and stripes. Let's focus on the choices we make because we are all cheetahs, after all."

The crowd nodded; they knew they were wrong. From then on, the cheetahs stopped listening to Bella's lies and chose to love and help each other instead.

Word of Rebel's speech spread all across Freedom Island, and one day, she received a mysterious letter.

Dear Rebel,

For the hurting, love takes more courage than hate.

Your determination to seek peace in Furenzy Park shows that you love justice more than revenge. Freedom Island needs animals like you to protect it from anger. If you are willing to defend our dear island, answer the call. Journey to Wizards Way by the first day of fall.

Hurry. So many animals are falling into hate.

Anticipating your speedy arrival—
The Legends of Freedom Island

Team BRAVE,

Bella is back at her nasty tricks. She's planning on cheating in the next Furenzy Race, and you must complete the three missions below to finish first:

- Prepare for the race by updating your map with the Rebel sticker included.

- Defeat Bella in the BRAVE Challenge, and celebrate your victory with an epic reward.

- Apply what you've learned by making your best friends a card, telling them what qualities make them special to you.

The outcome of the race is riding on you!
Are you ready to be BRAVE?

YOUR MISSION

TO YOUR FAMILY

INTRODUCTION

BRAVE Books has created the BRAVE Challenge to drive home key lessons and values illustrated in the story. Each activity (a game and the accompanying discussion questions) takes between 10 and 20 minutes. Family-focused and collaborative, the BRAVE Challenge is a quick and fun option for family game night.

BRAVE CHALLENGE KEY

 Read aloud to the children

 One child modification

 For parents only

 Roll the die for Bella

THE BRAVE CHALLENGE

 ## OBJECTIVE

Welcome to Team BRAVE! Your mission for this BRAVE Challenge is to win the Furenzy Fifty-Three. To get started, grab a sheet of paper and a pencil, and draw a scoreboard titled **Team BRAVE vs. Team Bella**, like the one shown.

Team Bella	Team BRAVE
|||	ᚦᚻᚻ ||

While the children create the scoreboard, decide on a reward for victory. Here are a few ideas:

- *Going on a walk or hike*
- *Going swimming*
- *Movie night*
- *Playing the children's favorite game*
- *Buying candy bars*
- *Riding bikes*
- *Whatever gets your kiddos excited!*

 # HOW TO PLAY

In this BRAVE Challenge, Team BRAVE (the children) will compete against Team Bella to earn points. At the end of all three activities, the team with the most points wins.

During each game the parent will roll a die for Bella. The number rolled will represent the number of points Bella earned in that game. Write this value on Bella's half of the scoreboard.

As you follow the instructions, Team BRAVE will also earn points. At the end of each game, write that value on the scoreboard under "Team BRAVE."

 # WINNING

At the end, if Team BRAVE has earned more points than Bella, then they have won the Furenzy Fifty-Three. The prize for winning will be _____. Let's begin!

INTRODUCING...

THE HODGETWINS

Kevin and Keith Hodge are conservative political commentators and popular influencers who have spent their career using humor to bring awareness to issues such as the dangers of Critical Race Theory. They helped BRAVE Books write this story and the BRAVE Challenge, and they'll be popping in to give you ideas on how you can explain these concepts to your child.

HODGETWINS SUGGEST

"Hi, parents! We hope your family has a great time during this BRAVE Challenge and makes all kinds of gains!"

CRITICAL RACE THEORY (CRT)

A theory claiming that a person's worth and social power is largely decided by his or her race, defining some racial groups as "oppressed" and others as "oppressors." They claim that this system of oppression is inherent in the American social and political structures. Often, white activists promote CRT trying to defend minorities.

GAME #1 - GRANNY OR BELLA SAYS

LESSON

It's important to listen to trustworthy people.

MATERIALS NEEDED

A six-sided die.

Video Tutorial

OBJECTIVE

Team BRAVE, as you prepare for the big race, both Rebel's granny and Bella are giving you advice. Your objective is to only listen to and follow Granny's instructions as best you can.

INSTRUCTIONS

*Before starting, roll the die to see how many points Team Bella earned. **Record this number on the scoreboard.***

1. Team BRAVE stands in a line.
2. When the parent says things like, "**Granny** says, touch your nose," Team BRAVE must follow the instruction.
3. When parents say things like, "**Bella** says, touch your toes," Team BRAVE should *not* listen to her.
4. Team BRAVE starts out with six points, and for each mistake, they will lose one point.

Game on!

Parents say:

- "Granny says, touch your nose."
- "Granny says, spin in a circle three times."
- "Bella says, jump on one foot."
- "Granny says, hop like a bunny."
- "Bella says, pick your nose."
- "Granny says, do your favorite dance move."
- "Granny says, crawl around like a worm."
- "Bella says, pat your head and rub your stomach at the same time."
- "Granny says, pat your head and rub your stomach at the same time."

─── **BRAVE TIP** ───
Parents can think of other silly commands to keep the game going.

TALK ABOUT IT

1. Remember how Granny and Bella each interacted with Rebel in the story. Why would you want to listen to Granny and not Bella?

2. What makes someone trustworthy?

3. Why is it important to listen to someone trustworthy, like Granny?

HODGETWINS SUGGEST

"Having someone you can trust or confide in is extremely important. You know they are for you and want to see you grow and succeed, so you don't have to question their motives when getting advice from them."

GAME #2 - CAN YOU HEAR IT?

LESSON

Learn to listen closely.

MATERIALS NEEDED

A six-sided die and 8-10 items from the room you are in.

Video Tutorial

 ## OBJECTIVE

The race is on! Team BRAVE, you must stay ahead of Bella by listening carefully and keeping up the pace. Without seeing the item, Team BRAVE must identify different objects by listening to the various sounds made with them.

 ## INSTRUCTIONS

 Roll the die to see how many points Team Bella earned. **Record this number on the scoreboard.**

Setup:

1. Grab 8-10 objects from around the room. Look for objects made of different materials, for example: pencils/pens, TV remotes, books, pillows, bottles, toys, etc.
2. Place the objects on a table where Team BRAVE can see them.
3. Team BRAVE should study the objects to remember them and then turn around, backs toward the objects.

Playing:

1. Pick one member of Team BRAVE, still facing away from the table.
2. Use one item on the table to make a noise: tapping it with your fingers, dropping it, hitting it against the table, etc.

3. The chosen BRAVE member must guess the item, based on the sound alone.

   a. If the first guess is correct, give BRAVE two points.

   b. If the second guess is correct, assign one point.

4. If neither the first nor second guess is correct, reveal the answer, move to the next BRAVE member, and do not assign any points.

5. Repeat this process four times only. If BRAVE has more than four members, give each BRAVE member a chance and take the top four scores. **Record the sum of these four scores on the scoreboard.**

Game on!

--- BRAVE TIP ---

To help with cleanup, have Team BRAVE put back all of the remaining items in under 30 seconds for one bonus point.

🔊 TALK ABOUT IT

1. Why was listening carefully important in this game? Why is listening important in your life (at home, at school, with friends, etc.)?

2. Do you think that there are people like Bella who want to trick you into believing lies?

3. If you hear something that might be a lie, what should you do? Who should you tell about it?

4. In the book, Bella said that striped cheetahs should give their trophies to the spotted runners. Do you think this is fair? Why?

HODGETWINS SUGGEST

"Bella convinced the other animals that the Stripes are cheaters just because they have stripes. That is a harmful lie. We should not judge others by their outward appearance, but how well they treat others and the decisions they make. Thankfully, Madi was able to listen closely and spot the lie."

GAME #3 - BANANA PEEL ALERT!

LESSON

Success comes to those who work hard.

Video Tutorial

MATERIALS NEEDED

A six-sided die and 10-12 wadded paper balls.

OBJECTIVE

It is the last lap of the Furenzy Fifty-Three, and the race is too close to call. Bella is determined to win and will do anything to get the upper hand—even if it involves throwing banana peels (paper balls) at Team BRAVE to slow you down! Your mission is to dodge the banana peels and beat Bella to the finish line.

 # INSTRUCTIONS

 Roll the die to see how many points Team Bella earned. **Record this number on the scoreboard.**

1. Team BRAVE stands in an open area with enough space for running in place.
2. Parents sit about five feet away from them, facing Team BRAVE.
3. Team BRAVE runs in place for the entire game.
4. Parents will toss wadded paper balls at Team BRAVE.
5. Team BRAVE must dodge the balls while running in place.
6. They start with 8 points and will lose a point each time they are hit.

Game on!

TALK ABOUT IT

1. Did you have to work hard to run in place during the whole game and dodge every paper ball? What was the result of working so hard?

2. Can you think of a time where you received or earned something because you worked hard for it? *(For example, earning good grades, or saving up for a new bike.)*

3. What's more important: working hard or looking a certain way? For example, let's say your parents wanted to hire someone to fix a clogged toilet in your house. Is it better they find someone who knows their stuff and works hard or find someone that has red hair to do it?

 HODGETWINS SUGGEST

"Different perspectives are always good to have, but when you have a job that needs to be done, you want someone that can do it with excellence."

4. Why is it important to work hard? What do you think could happen to a person that doesn't work hard?

TALLY ALL THE POINTS TO SEE WHO WON!

BRAVE SUMMARY

There are people like Bella that are trying to convince others that the color of their skin is what makes them who they are. We know that how you look on the outside does not determine who you are on the inside. Showing love to others is the most important. Who you are is so much more than the color of your skin, just like the cheetahs are more than their spots and stripes.